Blue Kangaroo belonged to Lily.
He was her very own kangaroo.
Sometimes, when Lily was showing off
and not doing as she was told, she would say,
"I'll show you, Blue Kangaroo!"
And Blue Kangaroo watched. What else could he do?

When Lily was at Aunt Jemima's house,
she saw some acrobatics on TV.
Lily thought it looked easy.
"I'll show you, Blue Kangaroo!" she said.

Emma Chichester Clark

For my friend,
Arthur William Wace

Collect all the fantastic books about Blue Kangaroo!

Where Are You, Blue Kangaroo?

It Was You, Blue Kangaroo!

What Shall We Do, Blue Kangaroo?

Merry Christmas, Blue Kangaroo!

Happy Birthday, Blue Kangaroo!

Come to School Too, Blue Kangaroo!

When I First Met You, Blue Kangaroo!

First published in hardback in Great Britain by Andersen Press Ltd in 2003
First published in paperback by Collins Picture Books in 2005
New edition published by HarperCollins Children's Books in 2009
This edition published in 2016

5 7 9 10 8 6 4

ISBN: 978-0-00-717894-0

Collins Picture Books is an imprint of HarperCollins Publishers Ltd.
HarperCollins Children's Books is a division of HarperCollins Publishers Ltd.

Text and illustrations copyright © Emma Chichester Clark 2003, 2016

Visit our website at: www.harpercollins.co.uk

Printed in China

"No, Lily! Don't do that!" cried Aunt Jemima.
But Lily went right on doing it.

And Blue Kangaroo watched.
What else could he do?

"Lily!" cried Aunt Jemima. "I told you not to!
Why can't you do as you are told?"

The next day, Lily went to a party where there was
a juggler. Lily thought it looked easy.
She said, "I'll show you, Blue Kangaroo!"
"Lily!" said her mother. "Sit down!"

"No! Lily!" cried her mother. "Stop it at once!"

And Blue Kangaroo watched.
What else could he do?

"You always go too far," said Lily's mother.
"When are you going to learn to do as you are told?"

Aunt Florence took Lily to the park.
They saw some boys doing tricks on their bikes.
Lily thought it looked easy.
"I'll show you, Blue Kangaroo!" she said.

"No, Lily!" cried Aunt Florence. "STOP! Come back here!"

Blue Kangaroo could
hardly bear to watch.
Could you?

"Lily!" cried Aunt Florence. "Lily! Stop!"
But even if Lily had wanted to, she couldn't.

"What are we going to do with you, Lily?" asked
Aunt Florence. "Why won't you do as you are told?"

When Lily got home, Uncle George was playing with
Lily's baby brother on the seesaw.
"Can I have a go?" asked Lily.

"Okay, Lily," said Uncle George, "but you must be careful.
Not too fast, or the baby will fall."
But Lily had an idea…

"I'll show you, Blue Kangaroo!" she cried.
"Lily?" said Uncle George. "No, Lily!
DON'T DO THAT!" he shouted.

"LILY! NO!" cried Uncle George…

…and Blue Kangaroo
closed his eyes tight.
What else could he do?

"I told her not to," said Uncle George.
"Where's Blue Kangaroo?" cried Lily.
But nobody was listening.

Lily's mother sent Lily to bed early.
"I've had enough of you," she said. "And I expect
Blue Kangaroo has had enough, too."
"But where is Blue Kangaroo?" cried Lily.

Blue Kangaroo was outside, hanging dangerously.
His arms were aching and he couldn't hold on any longer.

Suddenly,
he fell…

…crashing,
scraping…

…down,
down…

…down to the ground below.
Poor Blue Kangaroo examined his tail.
It was torn and the stuffing was coming out.

He didn't know what to do.
Perhaps Lily would know.
He began to hop across the lawn, towards the house.

Before he got very far, Lily's mother appeared with a torch.
"There you are!" she said.

She sewed up his tail and put a bandage on it.
"What a brave little kangaroo," said Lily's father.
"I'm not sure I would stay with Lily if I were him."

Blue Kangaroo thought about that, all night,
as he sat alone on the windowsill.
Would Lily stop showing off?
Would she ever do as she was told?
Should he give her another chance?
What should he do?

When Lily came down in the morning,
she ran towards Blue Kangaroo.
"No, Lily," said her mother. "You can't have him
until you've shown us that you can be good,
and do as you are told."

That day, Lily did everything she was told.
She brushed her teeth and tidied her room.
She ate her lunch and helped with the shopping.
And she didn't show off once.
"So, are you going to turn over a new leaf?" asked her mother.

"YES!" said Lily. "I'm going to be good and
new and do as I am told! I'll show you.
And I'll show *you*, Blue Kangaroo!"
And Blue Kangaroo believed her.
What else could he do?